The Web at Dragonfly Pond

By Brian "Fox" Ellis

Illustrated by Michael S. Maydak

Dawn Publications

Sing a frog song!
Brian "Fox" Ellis

Dedications

*To my father, who taught me a love of all things wild, and to my daughters,
who already feel at home in the wild!* — *BE*

To Wolf and Teal, and to their children who may come. — *MSM*

Library of Congress Cataloging-in-Publication Data

Ellis, Brian, 1962-
   The web at Dragonfly Pond / by Brian "Fox" Ellis ; illustrated by Michael
S. Maydak.
      p. cm.
   Summary: A boy goes fishing with his father, and describes the
interrelationships among the insects and animals he encounters, from the
mosquito that bites him to the dragonflies, bullfrogs, and fish that he
finally catches and eats. Includes facts about wetland species in the story.
   ISBN 1-58469-078-X (hardback) -- ISBN 1-58469-079-8 (pbk.)
 [1. Pond ecology--Fiction. 2. Ponds--Fiction. 3. Pond animals--Fiction. 4.
Ecology--Fiction.] I. Maydak, Michael S., ill. II. Title.
   PZ7.E4675Web 2006
   [Fic]--dc22

                            2005026484

Dawn Publications
12402 Bitney Springs Road
Nevada City, CA 95959
530-274-7775
nature@dawnpub.com

Printed in China
10 9 8 7 6 5 4 3 2 1
First Edition

Design and computer production by Patty Arnold, Menagerie Design and Publishing

Author's Note

Every bit of this story is true. It all happened to me as I've told it in the following pages. Well, almost. The only thing I changed is this: not everything happened all in one day. I put it together that way because it makes a better story. But all of it DID happen, and in fact it happens most every summer day on farm ponds and small lakes all over the world—wherever there are mosquitoes, dragonflies and people who fish!

I remember fishing with my dad when I was ten years old, and we were getting eaten alive by mosquitoes. When I complained, my dad said, "Son, do you like to fish? Do you like listening to the songs of birds and frogs?"

"Why, yes." I said.

"Well, go ahead and brush off those mosquitoes, but don't complain about them doing their job. They feed the fish, the birds, and the frogs."

I wanted to say, "Dad, what are you talking about?" but I said nothing.

As we were rowing around Dragonfly Pond in a johnboat, we drifted into the cattails. My dad quietly tapped me on the shoulder and pointed. Right there, right near our boat, an ugly dragonfly nymph was crawling out of the muddy water. She crawled up this cattail and cracked the back of her shell.

Right before our eyes, she squiggled out of her shell and became a beautiful creature of the air. This nymph, this ugly creature of the swamp, transformed herself into a big, beautiful dragonfly.

"Amazing!" I whispered to myself, watching closely.

As we watched, she pumped fluid into her wet, crinkly wings, stretching them out, and held her new wings out to dry. We could see right through them, except for the black lace that holds them together. When the sun hit them just right, her glassy wings bent a ray of light, so that we could see a rainbow of colors.

We watched, transfixed. As this dragonfly took wing and darted off, I began to think about what my dad had said about feeding mosquitoes.

The mosquitoes were everywhere. They were eating us alive. There one went with a drop of my blood! Flying slowly, her belly was big and round—full of my blood!

SNATCH! Just then a great big dragonfly snatched that mosquito right out of the air.

My dad once told me that a dragonfly is like a hawk of the insect world. They can fly fast, up to 60 miles an hour! Or like a helicopter, they can hover perfectly still. They have six legs, which hang like a basket to scoop up other flying bugs. He said that one dragonfly will eat a few hundred mosquitoes each day!

I like dragonflies!

As that dragonfly was buzzing around eating mosquitoes and deerflies and horseflies, she met another dragonfly. After awhile they flew together, with the tail of one touching the back of the other. Flying together, they buzzed by our boat near the cattails by the shore.

The dragonfly that had eaten the mosquito that had eaten me, flew off by herself and touched her tail to the water again and again. My dad told me she was laying eggs—more than a hundred of them! Soon there would be baby dragonflies.

I asked him, "Why does she lay so many eggs?"

He said, "Many of those eggs will not hatch. Many that do hatch, will not survive; they will be eaten by minnows and other bugs. Those that survive will shed their skins several times as they grow from small nymph to large nymph to adult. Eventually they will sprout wings and fly, like that dragonfly."

He paused, then added, "Think about it: you went through similar changes. You started as an egg in a wet watery world. You were born a cute little baby, kind of like a larva. You will grow up into a struggling adolescent, like that nymph. And someday you will sprout wings, learn to fly and become an adult!"

My dad liked to make these kinds of comparisons between our lives and the lives of our wild kin. Me? Like a dragonfly? I began to wonder . . . in what ways would I be transformed? How am I like that dragonfly?

When the dragonfly was through laying eggs, SLURP! A great big bullfrog lunged out of the shallows and swallowed her whole. This huge bullfrog feasted. This was the kind of frog that sings to you when the moon is full. The frog lives in two worlds. He swims in dark pools and leaps about upon the land at dusk.

He seems to sing to the moon, and probably hopes another frog will hear his song. But I like to think he also sings just because it feels good in his big bulgy throat.

After his feast, the frog went swimming away,
out among the cattails and lily pads, when—
SPLOOSH! A great big black bass, a large mouth
bass, came splashing up out of the water and
swallowed that bullfrog whole. The bass swam
off to the bottom to rest and digest the bullfrog
in his belly.

The loud splash caught our attention. My dad and
I looked at each other, then turned to watch the
ripples settle. We began to row towards those
ripples.

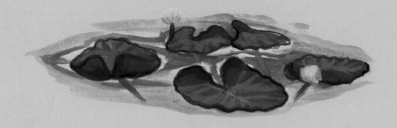

As we rowed across the pond, we watched the sun begin to set. Clouds were purple and pink, red and orange. The sun seemed to be setting into itself, reflecting in the calmness of the still water. I imagined rowing across a lake of fire. Sun fire, sky fire, earth fire, even the water seemed ablaze.

We saw a great blue heron stalking in the shallows for minnows and frogs. We saw a raccoon on the shore catching crawdads. A deer came to the bank to drink. A bald eagle circled high overhead. A black crow squawked as it flew towards the fiery western sky. We saw a spider spinning its web between two cattail stalks.

*More than a thought, I began to **feel** that somehow all of us were connected. Like invisible strands in a spider's web, there was something on that pond that bound us together. I took a deep breath and knew I was breathing in the breath of the willow trees.*

I saw a clear spot about the size of a basketball hoop, over near the shore, surrounded by cattails and duckweed.

This is the spot, something in me said. The weeds were a perfect place for the bass to hide, and the small pool of calm water was inviting.

I whispered, "Dad, that looks like the perfect place. If there is a big bass over there I am going to catch it!"

My dad chuckled. As if to challenge me, he asked, "Can you cast into that little spot from here?"

I said, "Watch!"

I tied on my favorite lure, a jointed minnow, hand carved of wood so it floats. It has a swivel in the middle of its back, so when you wiggle it, it swims like a wounded minnow.

My dad often talked about predator-prey relationships. He said that it is easier for a predator to catch a sick or wounded animal. This way they help the school of fish, herd of deer or flock of birds stay healthy. As my dad liked to put it, "I think there is an understanding between wolf and deer, heron and frog, spider and fly."

I stared at that spot where we saw the bass jump, concentrating, meditating.

I think I can, I think I can, I think I can. I know I can, I know I can, I know I can.

I cast ... I can! My lure landed right on the edge of that circle! My heart was pounding. My palms were sweaty.

Now my dad, who taught me everything I know about fishing, often said that when you cast a surface plug onto the water, you should let it sit there awhile so the fish get used to it. So I waited until the concentric circles disappeared.

I waited until the water was smooth as glass.

And I waited some more.

Then I wiggled it ... and wiggled it ... and ... nothing happened. The lure was tangled in the weeds.

I guess I should give up ...

SPLASH! A great big black bass came flying out of the water with my lure in its mouth! I set the hook! He dove down to the left trying to tangle me in the weeds! He swam underneath the boat, trying to get away!

As I wrestled with that big fish, it was as if everything moved in slow motion. Every thump of my heart, every breath, every moment, stretched as if time didn't exist.

My dad had always said that to be a better fisherman, you need to learn to think like the fish. Watching that big bass struggle for his life, I imagined the fear he must have felt. Knowing his life was in my hands, I felt my heart leap in my chest. I trembled for a moment.

"Dad, get the net ready!" I yelled. "He's a big one!"

"We don't have a net, son," he replied.

So I pulled the fish alongside the boat. My dad reached down and pulled him in.

That was the biggest bass I ever caught, even to this day!

My dad also taught me about catch and release. He would say, "It's a good idea to let a few go now and then. If you take away all of the predators, then the web of life will be out of balance. If you want fish again next year, you have to let a few go this year."

So we often let them go.

But not always. The fish we caught helped feed the family. We also grew most of our own vegetables and fruits in our backyard garden. Mom and dad made sure my brother and I knew where our food came from. We needed this fish for dinner, so we put him on the stringer and took him home.

When we got home my mom and brother said, "What did you catch? What did you catch?" Beaming with pride, I held up my bass. He weighed five and a half pounds. He was more than eighteen inches long.

As my dad began to filet the bass, he noticed a lump in the fish's stomach. "Let's see what this fish has been eating," he said. Inside the bass' belly we found a bullfrog. Inside the bullfrog, I imagined the dragonfly. Inside the dragonfly, I imagined a mosquito. Inside the mosquito, I imagined a drop of blood. A little bit of me!

That night at dinner, my hope was that something of the life of that bass would live in me. As I shared that fish with my family, I thought about the mosquito and the dragonfly, the frog and the bass, and I knew in my bones that dad was right.

In my blood flows the song of the birds, the buzz of mosquito. Inside me is the hum of the dragonfly's wing, the croak of the frog, and the splash of the large mouth bass. And because I fed a mosquito, something of my life flows in all of them.

A DAY ON DRAGONFLY POND

Inside this simple story are several main characters: mosquitoes, dragonflies, bullfrogs, a large mouth bass, and ME! The more we learn about the pieces, the more the whole web of life makes sense.

Mosquitoes (Culex pipiens) are one of the most important strands in this web of life. They are eaten by several creatures in the story. Dragonfly larvae eat mosquito larvae; adult dragonflies eat adult mosquitoes. (I like dragonflies!) Small minnows, frogs, and many birds eat them, too. Mosquitoes are one of the deadliest creatures on earth.

More people die each year from malaria and other diseases carried by mosquitoes than from shark bites or snake bites. But just as millions of people swim in the ocean and never are bitten, likewise millions of people are bitten by mosquitoes without getting sick. Take precautions, wear long sleeves and repellent, but don't let mosquitoes keep you indoors. As my dad says, "If you like to hear the birds singing, don't complain about the mosquitoes!"

Dragonflies really are my favorite insect, including the Green Darner Dragonfly (Anax junius) that is illustrated in this story. Dragonflies are the hawks of the insect world. They can fly 60 miles per hour, or hover in the same spot. About 200 million years ago, there was a super-sized dragonfly with a wingspan two to three feet across, about the size of a hawk today.

The dragonfly is also an aquatic "indicator species." They will tell you if a creek is clean or polluted. Visit your local creek or pond and look for bugs. If you find dragonfly nymphs and stone fly nymphs then it is clean. If you find no bugs in the water, it could be polluted. The kind of insects you find tell you about the quality of the water. You can be a science detective and help monitor your local watershed. Visit my website (www.foxtalesint.com) and click on the dragonfly to learn more about using dragonflies to monitor water quality.

Bullfrogs (Rana catesbeiana) are the largest frogs in North America. They have the deep baritone voice that you hear at night. Most frogs lay eggs that become adults within a few weeks, but the bullfrog tadpole will overwinter, becoming an adult the following spring. Frogs have a semi-permeable membrane, a wet skin that lets in some things and keeps out others. This makes them sensitive to chemicals in the environment. Frogs around the planet are becoming extinct. If you hear frog songs in your neighborhood, consider yourself lucky.

A group of students noticed that the frogs in their town were disappearing. They came up with a plan that has saved thousands of frogs and helped to clean up their environment. Here is what you can do. Go out in the spring with a tape recorder and record frog songs. Then compare the songs you recorded with songs you can download on the internet. By comparing your recording with the known species of your region, you can identify the species that live near you. You can send this information to your state Department of Natural Resources. This helps them to monitor frog populations. If you do this every year, you create a long range picture of the health of your local wetland. Visit my web page and click on the bullfrog for more information.

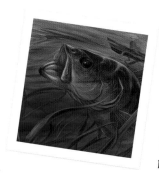

LARGE MOUTH BASS (MICROPTERUS SALMOIDES) is a favorite sport fishing species. As my father always said, "If you want to catch fish, think like a fish." To help you see the world through a fish-eye lens, here is a brief biography of the Large Mouth Bass.

Late in the spring the male bass uses his tail to hollow out a nest in the shallows. A female deposits as many as 5,000 eggs. The father guards the nest. The eggs hatch in two weeks. The embryonic fingerlings live off the yolk sac for another week. They eat insect larvae as their first meal. The adult male protects his young for their first three to four weeks. Their first year of life is the toughest. Most of them will be eaten by larger fish or wading birds. If they survive, they will grow to approximately six inches and weigh five to eight ounces by the end of their first year. With each year of growth they will add a new layer to their scales. Like counting tree rings, if you look at a fish scale with a magnifying glass you can estimate the age by counting rings. Within a few years the bass can grow to 18 to 24 inches and weigh 3 to 12 pounds. Bass have been known to live for 20 years and weigh as much as 25 pounds.

Like tigers, bass hunt by hiding in whatever cover is available—submerged logs, stumps, or weeds. When prey swims near, they lunge out and swallow it whole. They will eat almost anything, including insects, smaller fish, frogs, snakes, mice, even baby muskrats and ducklings!

CATTAILS (TYPHA LATIFOLIA) are one of the few plant species that are native all over the planet. Plants are the foundation of the food web. Through photosynthesis they harness sunlight and convert carbon to sugars. Plants also convert carbon dioxide to oxygen, which is essential for animal life. Many creatures depend on cattails for food. Insects eat the leaves. Muskrats eat the roots. People boil the roots like potatoes, and eat the fresh shoots like asparagus. Native Americans traditionally used cattail leaves to weave mats. These cattail mats were used for bedding, floor coverings, and walls on their wigwams. They are called cattails because the seed head looks like the plump tail of a cat. These seeds have a bit of fluff and are transported by wind.

HUMANS (HOMO SAPIENS) includes you and me. Here I am at age 8 with a Big Fish I caught. We are one of the most adaptable species on the planet. We live in almost every ecosystem. Fishing is a popular hobby and it is one way in which we provide food for our families. Some people eat frog legs. And of course, people are food for mosquitoes. We are part of the web of life.

What plants or animals are your favorite foods? Using my story as a model, write your own story about your adventures in the web of life. The food web is not just a concept in a science book—it is part of everyday life. Every time you eat, you are part of the food web. This very moment, as you read this book, there are tiny creatures living on your skin and hair, eating your dead skin. We continually make choices that affect the other creatures. We can pollute a stream—or we can plant willow trees along a creek to reduce erosion. We can pave a wetland—or we can monitor frog and insect populations to insure that the aquatic environment is healthy. The future of the web of life, our future, is in our hands.

Brian "Fox" Ellis is a professional storyteller, environmental educator, museum consultant, and Riverlorian for the Spirit of Peoria riverboat. His love for nature, for fishing, and for Midwest farm ponds grew from many an adventure with his father such as portrayed here. After listening to kids at camp whine about mosquitoes, he started telling this story in order to convey on a visceral level how all things in nature are important and how we humans are actively engaged in the web of life—even being food for mosquitoes. "Fox" still loves to fish on farm ponds near his home in Peoria, Illinois; so do his two daughters. This is his first book with Dawn Publications.

Michael S. Maydak is a professional artist who is passionate about nature—especially the riparian environments that he loves so much as a fly fisherman. He and his son, Wolf, often go fishing together. Mike is an art graduate of San Jose University and has been a professional artist since 1976, with his studio at his home in Cool, California. This is the fifth book he has illustrated for Dawn Publications.

OTHER BOOKS CELEBRATING THE WEB OF LIFE FROM DAWN PUBLICATIONS

Under One Rock (2001), *In One Tidepool* (2002), *Around One Cactus* (2003), *Near One Cattail* (2005), and *On One Flower* (Fall, 2006), each book exploring the community of creatures in particular habitats, by Anthony Fredericks, illustrated by Jennifer DiRubbio.

Eliza and the Dragonfly by Susie Rinehart, illustrated by Anisa Claire Hovemann, a charming story of a girl and a dragonfly, each experiencing their own metamorphosis. Winner of the 2005 International Reading Assn. award for picture books.

Salmon Stream by Carol Reed-Jones, illustrated by Michael S. Maydak, follows the dramatic lives of salmon from stream to ocean and back.

A Walk in the Rainforest (1992), *A Swim through the Sea* (1994), and *A Fly in the Sky* (1996), now-classics from the young author/illustrator Kristin Joy Pratt.

Dawn Publications is dedicated to inspiring in children a deeper understanding and appreciation for all life on Earth. View our complete catalog at www.dawnpub.com. Order online or call 800-545-7475.